A

ANTICS!

Z

ANTICS!

An Alphabetical **Ant**hology

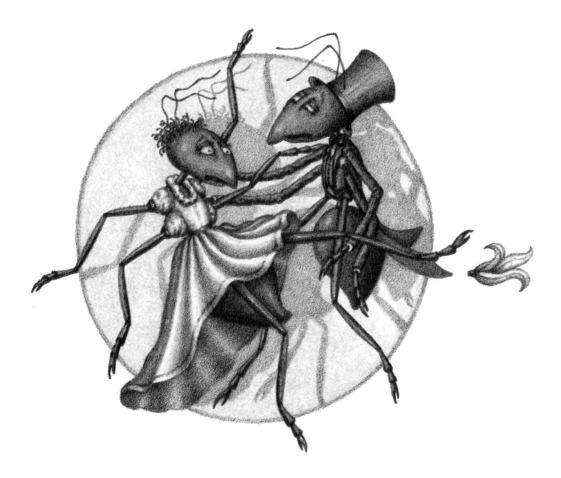

Cathi Hepworth

SCHOLASTIC INC.

New York Toronto London Auckland Sydney
Mexico City New Delhi Hong Kong

A

ISBN 0-439-13985-6

Copyright ©1992 by Catherine Hepworth.
All rights reserved.
Published by Scholastic Inc., 555 Broadway, New York, NY 10012,
by arrangement with Penguin Putnam Inc.
SCHOLASTIC and associated logos are trademarks
and/or registered trademarks of Scholastic Inc.

12 11 10 9 8 7 6 5 4 3 2   1 2 3 4/0

Printed in the U.S.A.   14

Z

For Brad,
and for Mom, Dad, Dave,
John, Jenni, Becki, and Ami…
"the Neandersons"

Antique

Brilliant

Chant

Deviant

Enchanter

Flamboyant

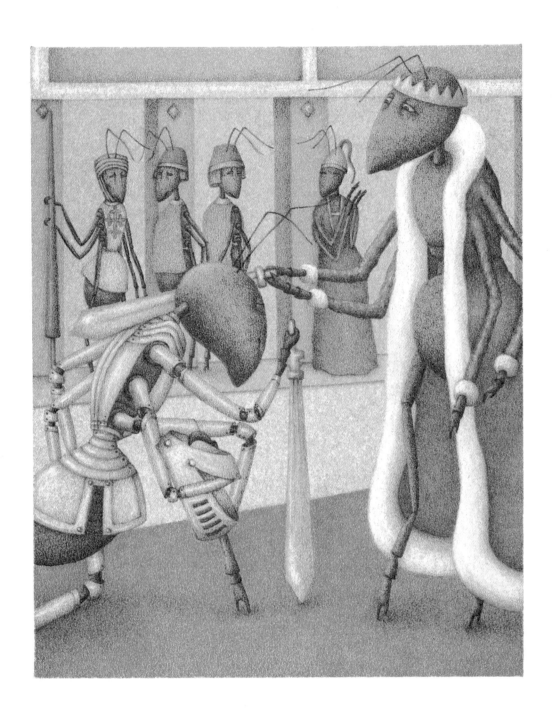

Gallant

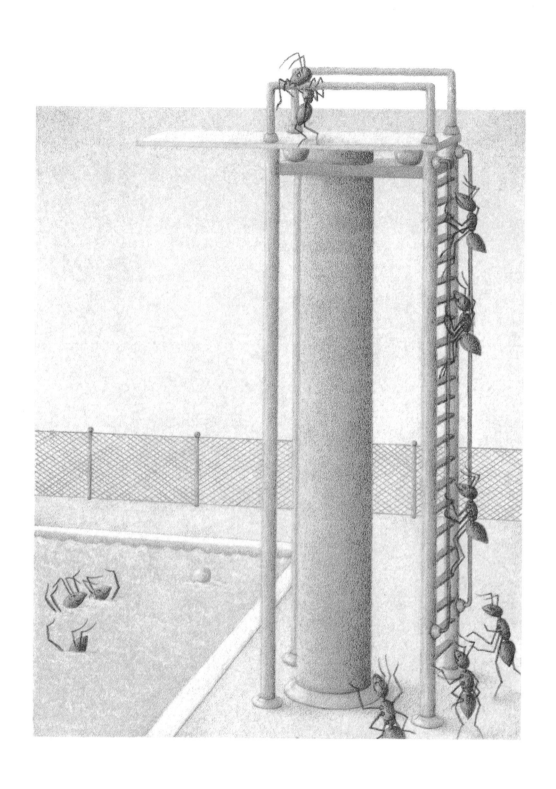

Hesitant

Immigrants

Jubil**ant**

Kant

Lieuten**a**nt

Mutant

N onchal**ant**

Observant

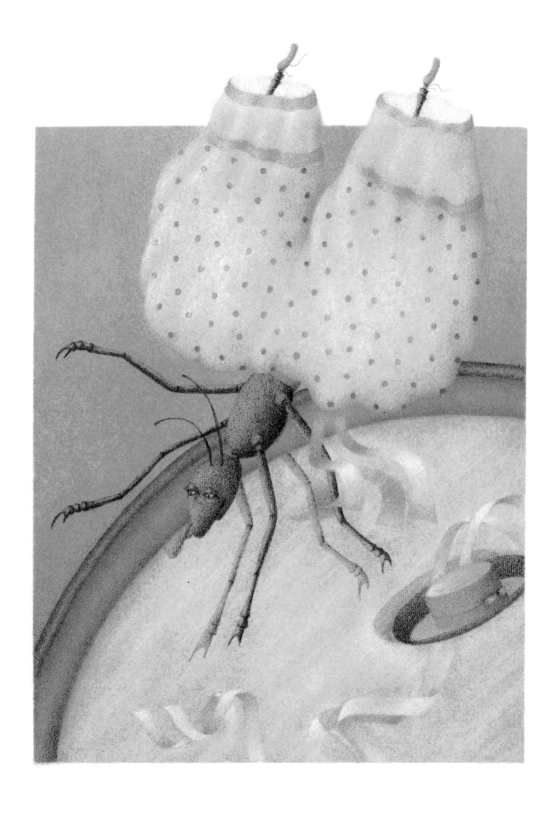

Pantaloons

Quarantine

Rembrant

Santa Claus

Tantrum

Unpleas**ant**

Vigil**ant**es

WANTED

THE OUTLAW

DANGEROUS "FIVE-LEGS" BOB

$5,000.00

for ARREST or CAPTURE

DEAD or ALIVE

LAST SEEN AT THE MAPLETON TOWN PICNIC
STEALING LARGE CRUMBS

Wanted

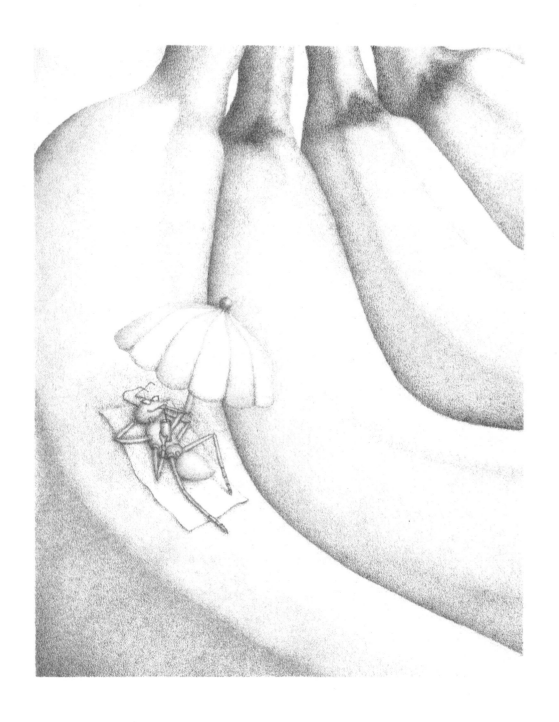

Xanthophile

Your **A**nt Yetta

AntzzzzzZ